D1218787

TREASURED TALES OF CHILDHOOD

Stories About People

Put together by
Barbara Simons and Ruth Rooney

Published by THE SOUTHWESTERN COMPANY *Nashville, Tennessee*

Stories About People

Contents

JACK and the Beanstalk

Illustrated by Anne Sellers Leaf

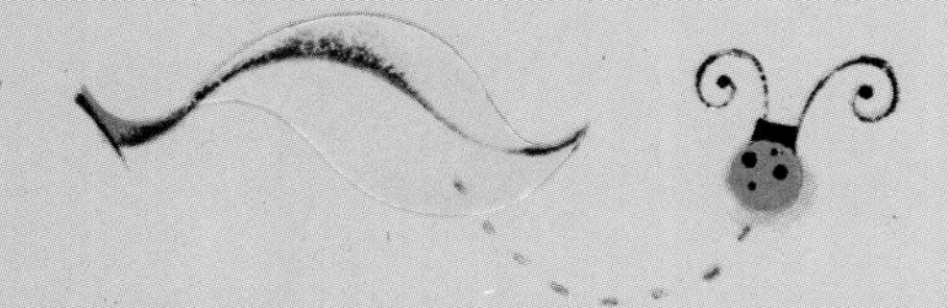

RAND McNALLY & COMPANY · Chicago

Established 1856

ONCE there was a poor widow who had an only son, named Jack. He was good-natured and affectionate but lazy. As time went on, the widow grew poorer and poorer until she had nothing left but her cow. And all the time, Jack grew lazier and lazier.

One day Jack's mother said to him, "To-morrow you must take the cow to market. The more money you get for her the better, for we have nothing left to live on."

Next morning Jack got up earlier than usual, hung a horn around his shoulder, and started out with the cow. On the way to market he met a queer little old man.

"Good morning, my lad," said the queer little old man. "Where may you be going with that fine cow?"

"I'm taking her to market," replied Jack.

"As if you had wit enough to sell cows! A bit of a lad that doesn't even know how many beans make five!"

"Two in each hand and one in your mouth," answered Jack, with a quickness that would have made his mother proud.

"Oho!" laughed the queer little old man. "Oho! Since you know beans, suppose you look at these," and he held out his hand, filled with rainbow-colored beans. "I'll give you all these for your cow."

"That would be a good bargain," thought Jack. So he traded the cow for the beans and hurried home.

"Look, Mother," he said gleefully, as he poured the beans into her lap. "I got all these pretty beans for the cow."

"You stupid boy!" she cried. "Now we shall have to starve." And she flung the beans out of the open window.

The next morning Jack woke early. He ran into the garden and found a beanstalk had sprung up during the night from the beans his mother had thrown away, and had grown so quickly its top was out of sight.

Jack began to climb, and he climbed and he climbed until he reached the top. He stepped

off into the sky and walked on until he met a beautiful woman with a face like a star.

Now the lady was a fairy and she knew what Jack was thinking and answered him without his asking any questions.

She told Jack he was in a country that belonged to a wicked Giant. This Giant had killed Jack's father and stolen all his gold and precious things. Jack had been only a baby at that time, and his mother had been too sad ever to talk to him about it.

"If you and your mother are ever going to be happy again," said the fairy, "you must punish that Giant." She whispered in Jack's ear, telling him what to do. Then she left and Jack walked on.

Toward evening he came to the door of a castle. He blew his horn, and a cook as broad as she was tall opened the door. "I am very tired and hungry," said Jack politely. "Can you give me supper and a night's lodging?"

"You little know, my poor lad, what you ask," she sighed. "A Giant lives here and he eats people. He would be sure to find you and eat you for supper. It would never do!" And she shut the door.

But Jack was too tired to go another step, so he blew his horn again, and when the cook

came to the door he begged her to let him in. She began to cry, but at last led Jack into the kitchen. Soon he was enjoying a good meal and quite forgetting to be afraid. But before he had finished there came a *thump, thump, thump* of heavy feet, and in less than no time the cook had popped Jack into the great oven to hide.

The Giant walked in sniffing the air. "Fe Fi Fo Fum! I smell the blood of an Englishman! Be he live or be he dead, I'll grind up his bones to make my bread!" he thundered.

"You are dreaming," laughed the cook, "but there is something better than dreams in this dish." So the Giant stopped sniffing and sat down to supper.

Through a hole in the oven Jack peeped out and watched the Giant eat. When all the dishes were empty, the Giant bade the cook, "Bring me my hen."

She brought a much-ruffled hen and put it

on the table. "Lay," shouted the Giant, and the hen laid a golden egg.

Again and again the Giant shouted his orders in a voice of thunder, and again and again the hen obeyed, till there were twelve golden eggs on the table. Then the Giant went to sleep and snored so loud that the house shook.

When the biggest snore of all had shaken Jack out of the oven, he seized the hen and ran off as fast as he could to the top of the beanstalk. He climbed quickly down and carried the wonderful hen to his mother. Day after day the hen laid its golden eggs, and by selling them Jack

and his mother might have lived in luxury all their lives.

But Jack kept thinking about that wicked Giant who had killed his father, and of the fairy's command. So one day he climbed the beanstalk again. This time he had dressed himself to look like a different person, as he did not want the cook to know him. And, sure enough, when the woman came to the door, she did not recognize the lad she had hidden in the oven.

"Please," said Jack, "can you give me food and a place to rest? I am hungry and tired."

"You can't come in here," answered the cook. "Once before I took in a tired and hungry young

runaway, and he stole my master's precious hen that lays golden eggs."

But Jack talked to the cook so pleasantly that she thought it would be unkind to grudge him a meal. After Jack had a good supper, the

cook turned over an empty kettle and hid him under it. And it was none too soon, either, for in stalked the Giant, *thump, thump, thump* sniffing the air. "Fe Fi Fo Fum! I smell the blood of an Englishman! Be he live or be he dead, I'll grind up his bones to make my bread!" he bellowed.

"Stuff and nonsense," laughed the cook. And she placed his supper on the table.

After supper the Giant shouted, "Fetch me my harp." And the cook brought in a beautiful harp with strings of pure gold.

"Play!" commanded the Giant, and the harp began to play all by itself. Soon the Giant's snores drowned the sweet music. Then Jack jumped from under the kettle and seized the harp. But no sooner had he slung it over his shoulder than it cried out, "Master, Master!" For it was a fairy harp.

Jack was frightened and ran for his life toward the top of the beanstalk. He could hear the Giant running behind him, *thump, thump, thump*. Jack reached the top of the beanstalk and slid down it as quick as lightning, calling out as he went, "Mother, Mother! The ax, the ax!"

Jack's mother, holding out the ax, met him as he touched the ground. There was no time to lose, for the Giant was already halfway down. With one slashing blow Jack cut the beanstalk. There was a crash, and the Giant lay at his feet in the garden. Then Jack told his mother all the story. And as for the wonderful beanstalk it never grew again.

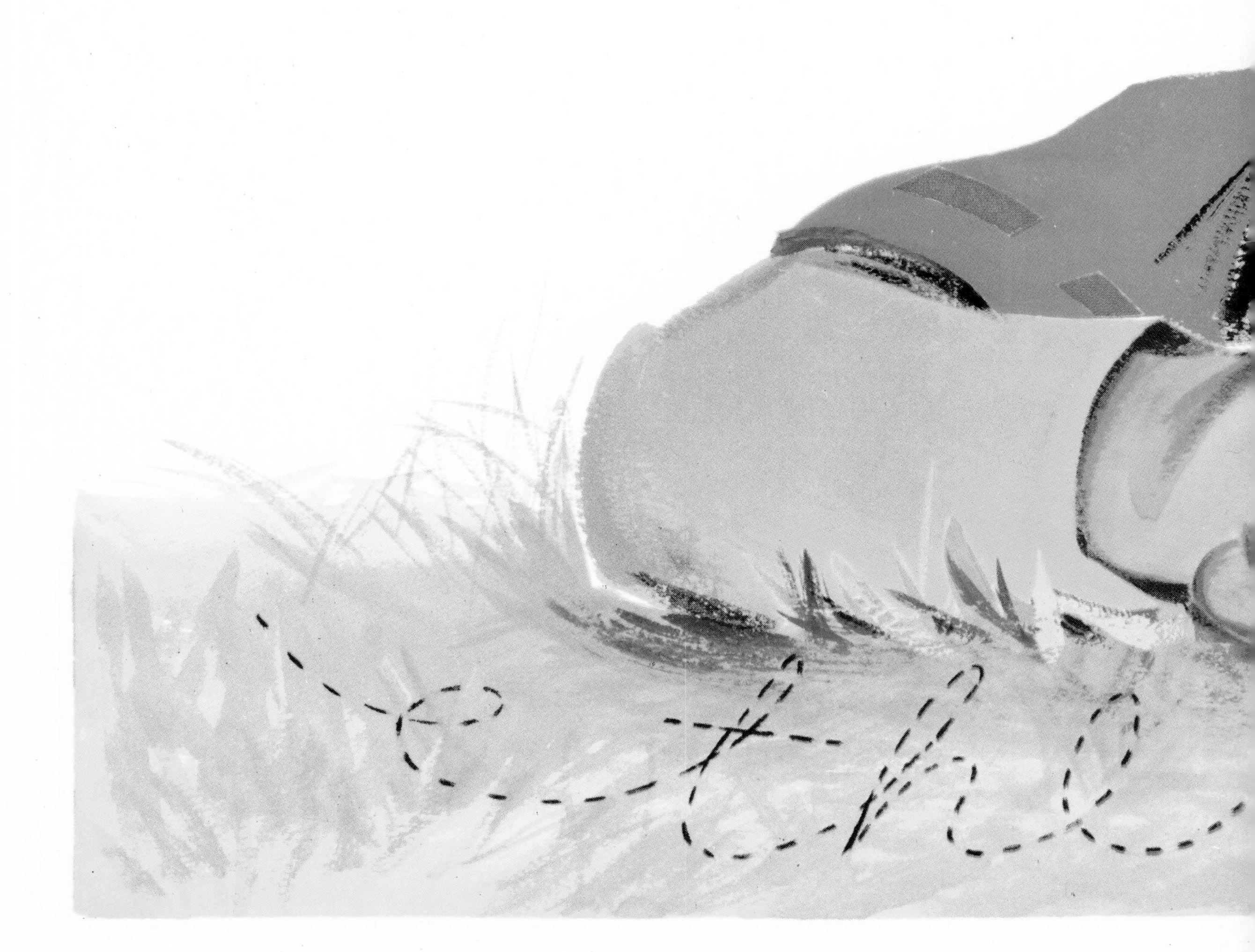

and

Rumpelstiltskin

Illustrated by ELIZABETH WEBBE

RAND McNALLY
& COMPANY

CHICAGO

Established 1856

ONCE THERE WAS a poor miller who had a beautiful daughter of whom he was very proud. One day he foolishly told the King his daughter could spin gold out of straw. The King loved gold above everything else, and he commanded that the maiden be brought to the castle.

When she arrived she was led to a large room half-full of straw. She was placed before a spinning wheel. The King said to her, "If all this straw is not spun into gold by morning, you shall die." He went out, and locked the door behind him with a huge key.

The poor girl sat down in a corner of the room and began to cry. She knew that she could not spin straw into gold.

Suddenly the door opened just a crack and a strange little man squeezed into the room.

"Good day, miller's daughter," he said. "What are you crying about?"

“Ah, me!” she sobbed, “I must die on the morrow, for I know not how to spin this heap of straw into gold.”

“What will you give me if I spin it for you?” asked the little man.

“This necklace I am wearing,” replied the maiden.

The little man agreed and, sitting down at the wheel, spun it around merrily—*whirr*, *whirr*, *whirr*. By morning the straw was gone and in its place was the gold. Then he twisted the necklace twice around his waist, and left as silently as he had come in.

When the King came next morning, he was pleased to see the gold, but he wanted more. He led the girl to a larger room, two-thirds full of straw, and ordered her to spin it all into gold before sunrise.

And again the maiden began to cry, and again the little man slipped through the crack of the door and said, "What will you give me, miller's daughter, to spin your straw into gold?"

"This ring on my finger," she replied.

So the droll little man set the wheel whirring again, twice as fast as before, and by daylight the straw was all spun into gold. Then he put on the ring and was gone.

The King came at dawn and was delighted to see the store of gold, yet his greedy heart was not satisfied. He took the miller's daughter into a vast chamber packed to the ceiling with straw. "Spin all this straw into gold this night," he said, "and tomorrow you shall be my queen."

As soon as the maid was alone, the queer little man appeared again and said to her, "Now what shall I have this time for my labor?"

"I have nothing more to give you," sighed the maiden.

"Then promise me your first child after you become queen," said the little man.

The maiden knew no other way out of her trouble, and promised to do what was asked.

That night the wheel whirred thrice as fast as before, and when the sun shone into the chamber, all the straw was gold.

The King was delighted to find all the straw spun into gold and, as he had promised, that very day he made the miller's daughter his queen.

At the birth of her first child the Queen was overjoyed. She had quite forgotten the queer little man until the day he slipped into her chamber and said, "Where is the child you promised me for spinning the King's straw into gold?"

The Queen wept bitterly and begged him not to take her baby. At last his odd little heart softened and he said, "I will give you three days to guess my name. If you can do it, you may keep the child." Then he slipped out of the room as quickly as he had come in.

The next day when the little man came, the Queen gave him the names of all the kings and princes that she could think of. But to all of them he gleefully answered, "Ho, ho! No, no, my Royal Dame! That's not my name! That's not my name!"

The next day the Queen sent messengers throughout the kingdom to collect all the curious names of poor folk. And when the little man skipped in, she began with Cow-ribs, Bandy-legs, Spindle-shanks, Snub-nose, and so on. But to all of them the little man shouted, "That's not my name!"

The third day the last of the messengers came back and said, "Forgive me, sorrowful Queen. I could find no new name but one. Yesterday, as I was passing through a strange wood, where foxes and hares say good-night to each other, I saw a small hut and in the doorway a funny little man sang this song,

" 'Today I bake, tomorrow I brew,
Today for one, tomorrow for two.
For how should she learn, poor Royal Dame,
That Rumpelstiltskin is my name?' "

When the Queen heard this, she knew the singer must have been her little gold-spinner.

At sunset the little man came skipping in and said, "Tell me my name if you can."

"Is it Hans?" she teased.

"No."

"Well, then, can it be Rumpelstiltskin?"

"The fairies have told you! The fairies have told you!" shrieked the little man in a rage, and he stamped his right foot so deep down through the floor that he could not pull it out. Becoming more angry still, he laid hold of his left foot with both hands and jerked so hard that he split himself in two, for he was really made of gingerbread, as are all Rumpelstiltskins.

THE PRINCESS WHO NEVER LAUGHED

illustrated by Marcia Grunewald

Printed in the U.S.A. by Western Printing and Lithographing Company

Once upon a time, in a castle made of marble and moonstone, there lived a lovely princess.

She was the most beautiful princess who ever lived,

and the gentlest,

the kindest,
and the wisest, too.

Yet, for all her goodness, she brought sorrow to those who loved her best. For this beautiful, gentle princess had never smiled.

Not as a baby when her royal mother brought her a new toy.

Not as a child when her royal father took her to the circus.

And not as a grown-up princess, when suitors came from far and wide to ask for her hand in marriage.

One day the king came out on his balcony and made a speech.

"It is the greatest wish of my heart that the princess be happy," he said. "I shall give her hand in marriage, and half my kingdom, to the man who can teach her eyes to sparkle and her lips to smile."

From that day forward hundreds of suitors came from all over the world.

One came dressed as a clown and jumped headfirst into a bucket of water. He looked very funny indeed.

"Poor fellow," said the princess, with tears in her eyes.

Another rode up to the castle on a polar bear's back.

A third pulled thirteen rabbits from his hat.

And a fourth told such a silly story that the king nearly burst with laughter.

For many days they came, and the princess talked to all of them very sweetly and solemnly. Often she wept to think how she must disappoint them.

One day a young fellow called Dummling heard of the king's offer. He was only a miller's son, and not very handsome, but he started at once for the castle.

On the way he met a little old man with a long beard.

"I am hungry, young sir," cried the old man. "Will you give me some bread?"

Dummling had only a crust for himself, but he was a good fellow, and he gave the bread to the beggar. At once the old man disappeared, and in his place stood a shining golden goose.

"Ho ho!" laughed Dummling. "Here's a fine gift to take to the princess!" And he picked up the goose and went on his way.

Soon he met three sisters who stared greedily at the golden goose. No sooner had Dummling passed by, than the eldest girl tried to snatch a feather from the bird. To her astonishment she stuck fast and could not let go, no matter how she tried.

"Stop!" cried the second girl and seized her sister's arm, whereupon she, too, was held fast.

A moment later the third sister had joined the chain and was being dragged helter-skelter down the road toward the king's castle.

After a bit they met a parson.

"Stop at once, you naughty girls," cried the old man, and he grasped the youngest sister's sleeve. And now he, too, was carried along.

By the time Dummling reached the castle there were, besides the three sisters and the old parson, a butcher, a baker, a farmer, and the farmer's wife, all hopping and tumbling along behind the golden goose. They were the strangest-looking crew in the world.

It happened that the princess was on the balcony enjoying the sun and crying contentedly as Dummling came up the road.

She looked once, and dried her tears.

She looked again, and her eyes sparkled merrily.

She looked once more, and the corners of her mouth turned up.

And then — and then *the princess laughed!*

"She laughed! The boy has made her laugh!" shouted the king, and he jumped up and down in delight.

"The princess laughed!" shouted all the courtiers.

"I laughed!" exclaimed the princess, and she did it again, just to be sure.

Within a very few days the king kept his promise, and a great wedding was held in the castle. Music filled the air, bells pealed across the land, and even the birds joined in a wedding song. But the loveliest sound of all, so everyone said, was the bright and joyous laughter of their happy princess.

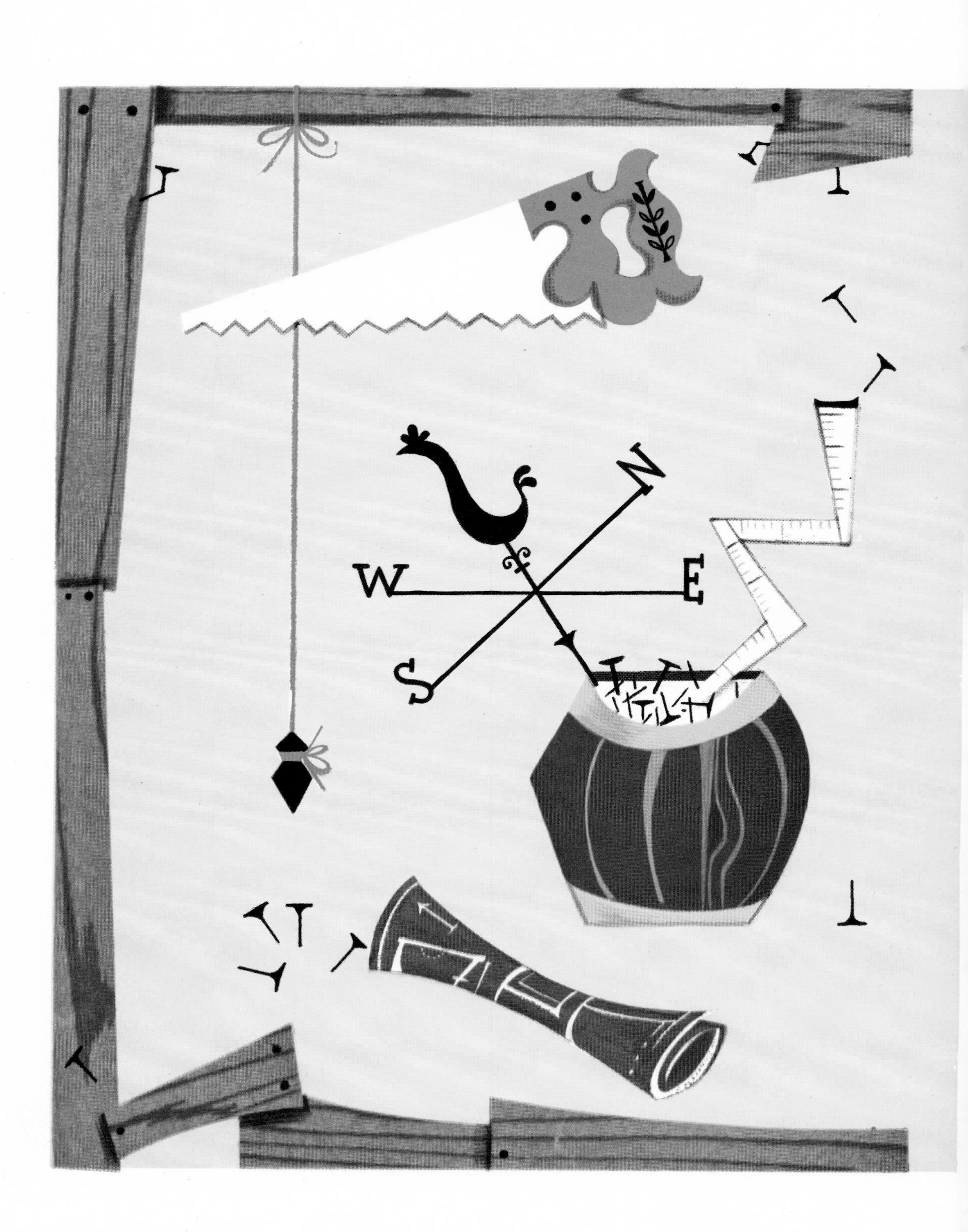
N
W
E
S

The House That Jack Built

Illustrated by

ANNE SELLERS LEAF

RAND McNALLY & COMPANY · Chicago
Established 1856

THIS IS the house that Jack built.

This is the malt
That lay in the house that Jack
built.

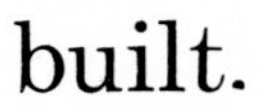

This is the rat,
That ate the malt
That lay in the house that Jack
built.

This is the cat,
That killed the rat,
That ate the malt
That lay in the house that Jack
built.

This is the dog,
That worried the cat,
That killed the rat,
That ate the malt
That lay in the house that Jack
built.

This is the cow with the crumpled
horn,
That tossed the dog,
That worried the cat,
That killed the rat,
That ate the malt
That lay in the house that Jack
built.

This is the maiden all forlorn,
That milked the cow with the
crumpled horn,
That tossed the dog,
That worried the cat,
That killed the rat,
That ate the malt
That lay in the house that Jack
built.

This is the man all tattered and
torn,
That kissed the maiden all forlorn,
That milked the cow with the
crumpled horn,
That tossed the dog,
That worried the cat,
That killed the rat,
That ate the malt
That lay in the house that Jack
built.

This is the priest all shaven
and shorn,
That married the man all
tattered and torn,
That kissed the maiden all forlorn,
That milked the cow with the
crumpled horn,
That tossed the dog,
That worried the cat,
That killed the rat,
That ate the malt
That lay in the house that Jack
built.

This is the cock that crowed in
the morn,
That waked the priest all
shaven and shorn,
That married the man all
tattered and torn,
That kissed the maiden all forlorn,
That milked the cow with the
crumpled horn,
That tossed the dog,
That worried the cat,
That killed the rat,
That ate the malt
That lay in the house that Jack
built.

This is the farmer sowing the
corn,
That kept the cock that crowed
in the morn,
That waked the priest all
shaven and shorn,
That married the man all
tattered and torn,
That kissed the maiden all forlorn,

That milked the cow with the
crumpled horn,
That tossed the dog,
That worried the cat,
That killed the rat,
That ate the malt
That lay in the house that Jack
built.

The Boy at the Dike

illustrated by Marguerite Scott

WHITMAN PUBLISHING COMPANY
Racine, Wisconsin
Printed in U.S.A.

Once upon a long-ago time, in a faraway land, there lived a not-quite-big-enough boy. The land was called Holland and the not-quite-big-enough boy was called Peter.

Peter helped his mother. He always dusted the bottom of the blue chest.

And he always dusted the legs of the table and chairs.

But when he tried to dust the tops of things, his mother always said, "Peter, you are not quite big enough to do that. Thank you for helping me. Now run along."

Peter liked to help his father. He helped him harness the dogs to the milk cart. But when he tried to help load the cart, his father, too, always said, "You are not quite big enough for this job, Peter. Now run along and play."

"They always say I am not quite big enough!" Peter said to himself. "But some day I will show them that I am *exactly* big enough!"

One day Peter's mother called to him. "Peter," she said, "will you carry this basket of gingerbread to Aunt Trinka? And be sure to hurry home before dark."

Peter put on his warm blue coat, buttoned its silver buttons, picked up the basket, and hurried off. He sang a funny little tune, "Aunt Trinka's . . . Aunt Trinka's . . . going to Aunt Trinka's. . . ."

On the way
Peter played his
favorite game. He
climbed to the top
of the dike, the
high bank that
held back the sea.

Without the dike
all of Holland
would have been
under water!
From the path on
the dike he
counted the
ships at sea.

Then he slid back down to the road. His wooden shoes sounded *clop cloppity clop* as he skipped along.

Not far from home Peter saw his cousin Gretel tending her geese. "Oh-ho, Gretel!" he shouted. "See me today! I am going to Aunt Trinka's all by myself!"

Gretel smiled and waved at Peter.

Farther on, Peter saw his Uncle Hans. "Helloo-oo, Uncle Hans," he called. "Today I am going to see Aunt Trinka *all by myself!*"

"Ach, now," Uncle Hans laughed, tossing him a juicy, yellow pear, "you are indeed getting to be a big boy, Peter."

After that, Peter saw nobody.

Suddenly, as he skipped along on the road next to the dike, he heard something. He heard a splashy trickly kind of noise. It sounded like water dripping. It *was* water dripping! But where could it be?

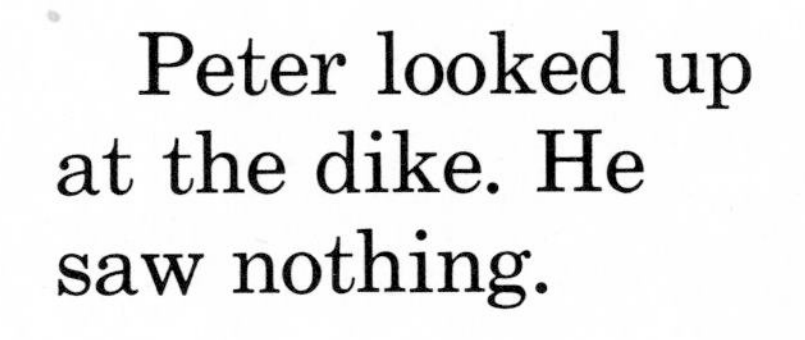

Peter looked up at the dike. He saw nothing.

He looked behind him. Nothing.

And then, looking a little way ahead, he saw — a hole in the dike!

Peter gasped. "If the hole is not closed up," he said aloud, "water will soon cover the land! Whatever shall I do?"

And even as he watched, the puddle grew larger. Then Peter had an idea. He took off his fine blue coat and folded it.

He put his hand into the hole. And then the water stopped trickling through it.

"I have found a way! I have found a way!" Peter said aloud. "Now the sea cannot come in through the hole. I will stay here until somebody comes along who can fix the dike."

Peter waited and waited. But nobody passed by on the lonely road. He put his hand even more firmly into the hole. "Soon now," he said, "soon somebody must come along."

Long shadows stretched out on the ground as the sun went down. And still Peter waited.

At last darkness covered the land. The friendly stars twinkled overhead. Peter nibbled on a tiny bit of Aunt Trinka's gingerbread.

He looked up at old Father Moon. "Surely someone will pass by soon," he said, yawning, "for I am becoming quite sleepy. . . ." His head nodded.

Suddenly a bright light awakened Peter. He heard the sound of many voices. Opening his eyes he saw his father and his mother and everybody in the village. They had all come looking for him.

"Look!" said Gretel. "Here is a hole in the dike! Peter stopped the water from coming in and flooding our land!"

"And," said Uncle Hans, "his hand was just big enough to fill the hole until it could be fixed!"

"He was just big enough," said the schoolmaster, "to know how very important it was to stop up such a dangerous hole!"

"Why," finished the mayor of the village, "Peter was just big enough to save us all!"

Perched on his father's shoulder, Peter smiled sleepily as the men of the village started to fix the hole in the dike.

And later, snuggled down into his own warm featherbed, he smiled again. "Oh, it is a *fine* thing," he whispered to himself, "to be a just-big-enough boy!"

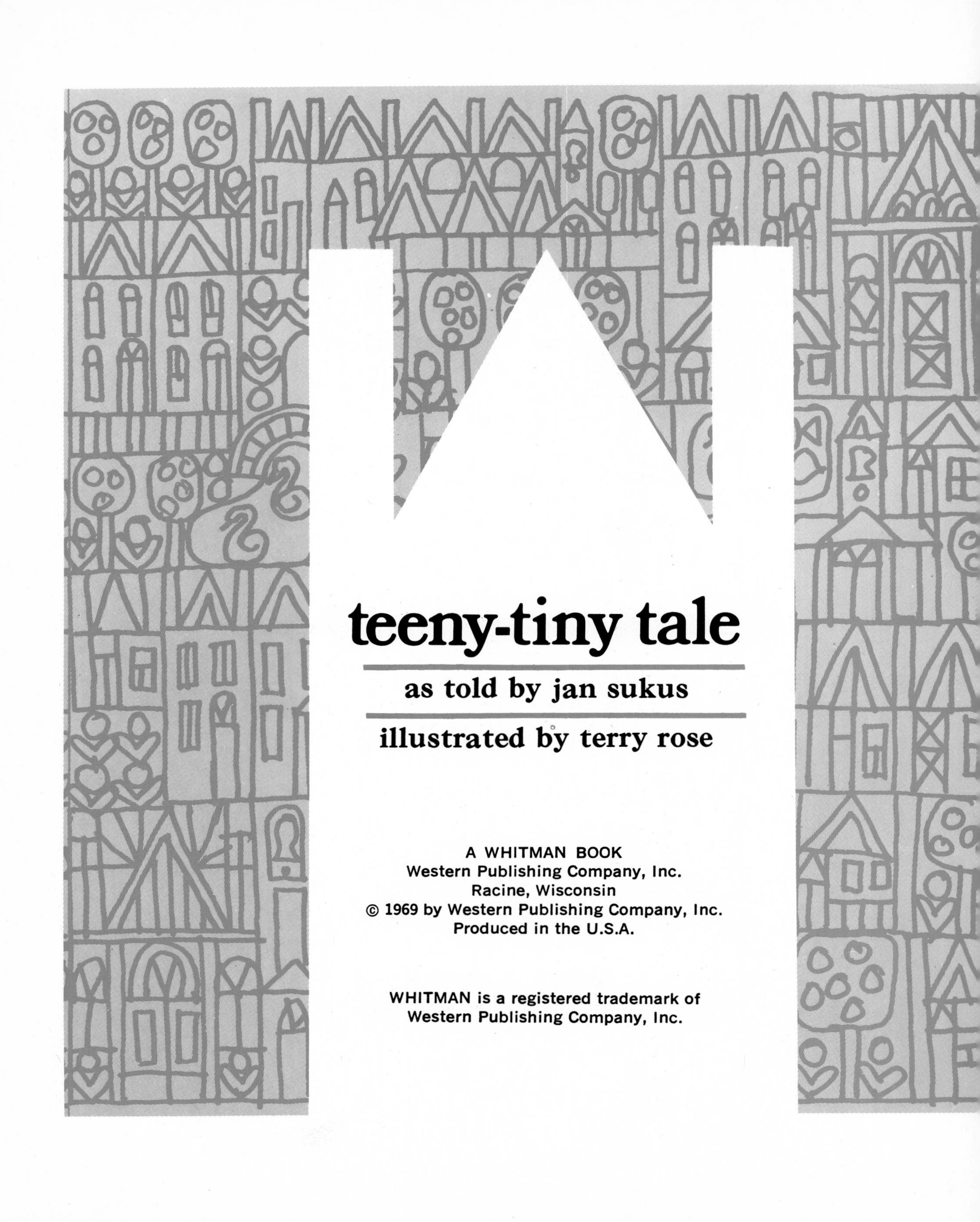

teeny-tiny tale

as told by jan sukus

illustrated by terry rose

A WHITMAN BOOK
Western Publishing Company, Inc.
Racine, Wisconsin

Produced in the U.S.A.

Once upon a time there was a teeny-tiny woman. She lived in a teeny-tiny town with her teeny-tiny cat in a teeny-tiny house.

One day the teeny-tiny woman cleaned her house. Then she said to the teeny-tiny cat, "I am a teeny-tiny bit hungry. I think I shall go out to find something for my teeny-tiny supper."

So she put on her teeny-tiny hat, took her teeny-tiny purse, patted her teeny-tiny cat, and then she walked out of her teeny-tiny house.

The teeny-tiny cat gave a teeny-tiny "Mee-ow," curled up on her very own teeny-tiny cushion, and took a teeny-tiny nap while the teeny-tiny woman went shopping.

When the teeny-tiny woman had gone a teeny-tiny way, she came to a teeny-tiny gate. She opened the gate quickly and walked into a teeny-tiny garden.

SPOT

In the garden she saw a teeny-tiny doghouse. Near the doghouse was a teeny-tiny bone.

"Ah!" said the teeny-tiny woman. "What a lovely bone! I will take it home and make some good soup for my teeny-tiny supper."

So she put the teeny-tiny bone into her teeny-tiny purse and went back to the house in the teeny-tiny town.

By
this time
the teeny-tiny
woman was too tired
to make the soup. So she put
the teeny-tiny bone into her teeny-
tiny kitchen cupboard and went up her
teeny-tiny stairs to her teeny-tiny bed.

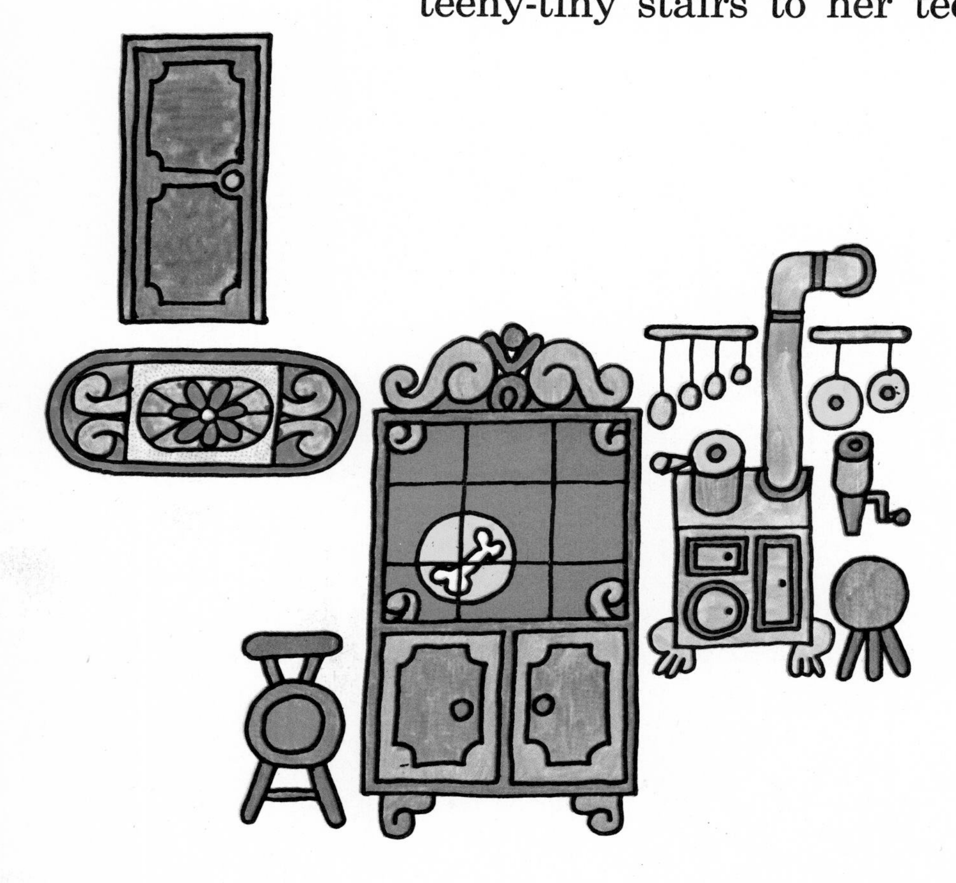

"I shall have a teeny-tiny nap," she said to her teeny-tiny cat.

But soon the teeny-tiny woman was awakened from her sleep by a teeny-tiny voice which said:

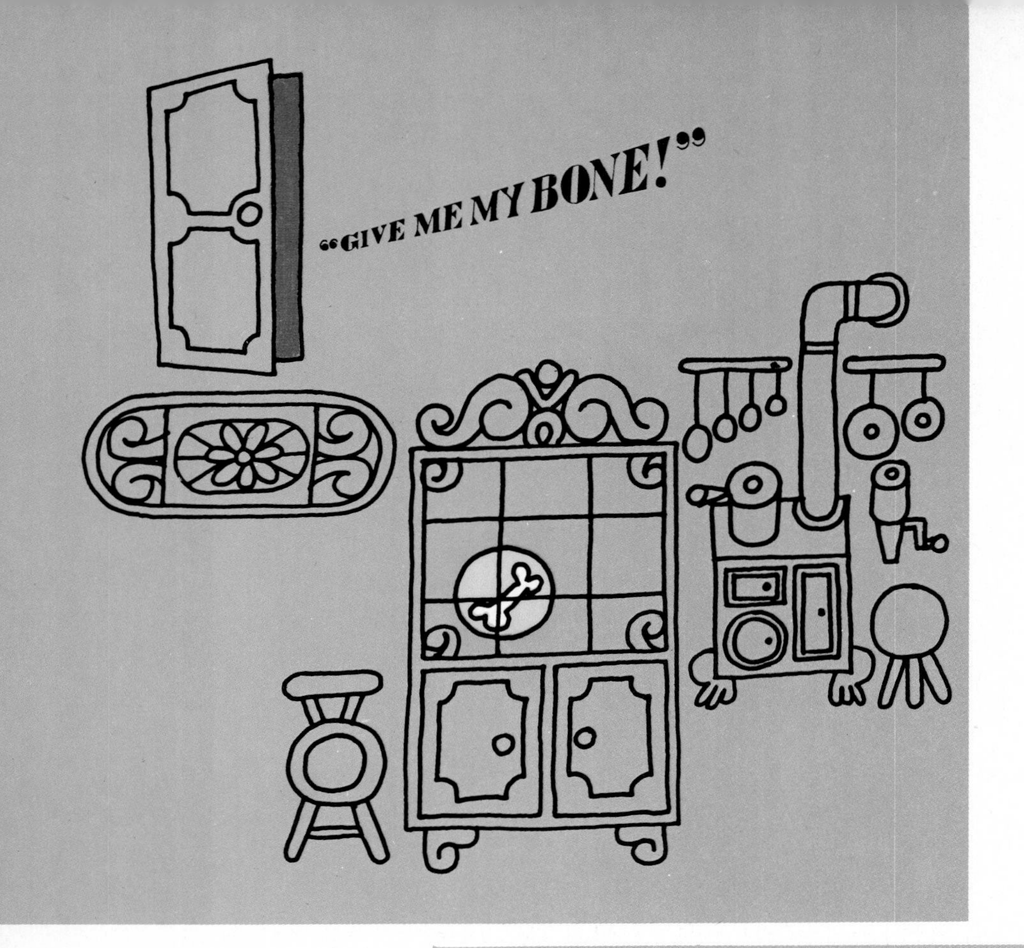

The teeny-tiny woman was just a teeny-tiny bit frightened. She covered her teeny-tiny head with her teeny-tiny blanket and fell asleep again.

When she had been asleep just a teeny-tiny time, she heard the voice again. This time it was a teeny-tiny bit louder:

This made the teeny-tiny woman a teeny-tiny bit more afraid. She covered her teeny-tiny head a teeny-tiny bit more with the teeny-tiny blanket.

When she had been asleep just a teeny-tiny bit longer, she heard the voice again. This time it was a great enormous voice:

The teeny-tiny woman was a teeny-tiny bit more frightened. She stuck her teeny-tiny head out from underneath the teeny-tiny blanket and said in her loudest teeny-tiny voice . . .

"TAKE

T!!!"

ILLUSTRATED BY Mary Stevens

Nobody Listens to Andrew

by Elizabeth Guilfoile

Follett Publishing Company
Chicago New York

Manufactured in the United States of America. Published simultaneously in Canada by The Ryerson Press, Toronto.

Library of Congress Catalog Card Number: 57-11019

Andrew saw something upstairs.
He ran down very fast.
He said,
"Listen, Mother."

Mother said,

"Wait, Andrew.

I must pay Mrs. Cleaner.

She must catch the bus before dark."

Andrew said,

"Listen, Daddy.

I saw something upstairs."

Daddy said,

"Wait, Andrew.

I must cut the grass before dark."

Andrew said,

"Listen, Ruthy.

I saw something upstairs.

It was in my bed."

Ruthy said,

"Wait, Andrew.

I must put on my roller skates.

I want to skate before dark."

Andrew said,

"Listen, Bobby.

I saw something upstairs.

It was in my bed on the sun porch."

Bobby said,

"Don't bother me, Andrew.
I must find my bat and ball.
I want to play ball before dark."

Andrew said,

"Listen, Mr. Neighbor.
I saw something upstairs.
It was in my bed on the sun porch.
It was black."

Mr. Neighbor said,
"Never mind, Andrew.
I must take my dog for a walk
before dark."

Andrew said very loud,
"Listen, Mother,
Listen, Daddy,
Listen, Ruthy,
Listen, Bobby,
Listen, Mr. Neighbor,
Listen, Mrs. Cleaner,
THERE IS A BEAR UPSTAIRS
IN MY BED."

Mother stopped paying Mrs. Cleaner.

She said, "Call the police!"

Daddy stopped cutting the grass.

He said, "Call the fire department!"

Bobby stopped playing ball.

He said, "Call the dog catcher!"

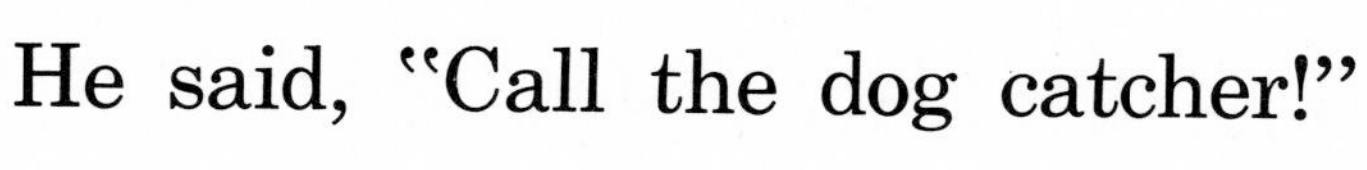

Ruthy stopped skating. She said,
"Call the zoo!"

Mr. Neighbor stopped taking his dog for a walk.

He called the police.
He called the fire department.
He called the dog catcher.
He called the zoo.

"Zoom!" came the police.
"Zing!" came the fire department.
"Whoosh!" came the dog catcher.
"Swish!" came the man from the zoo.

They all ran upstairs.

"Look!" said Mother.
"It is on the sun porch."
"Look!" said Daddy. "It is black."
"Look!" said Bobby.
"It is on Andrew's bed."
"Look!" said Ruthy. "It is a bear.
Andrew said it was a bear.
But nobody listens to Andrew."

The dog catcher caught the bear
in his net.
The fireman said,
"It climbed up the tree.
It climbed in the window."

The man from the zoo said,
"It is dry in the woods.
The bears are thirsty.
They are looking for water.
I will take this bear to the zoo."
Daddy said,
"Next time we will listen to Andrew."

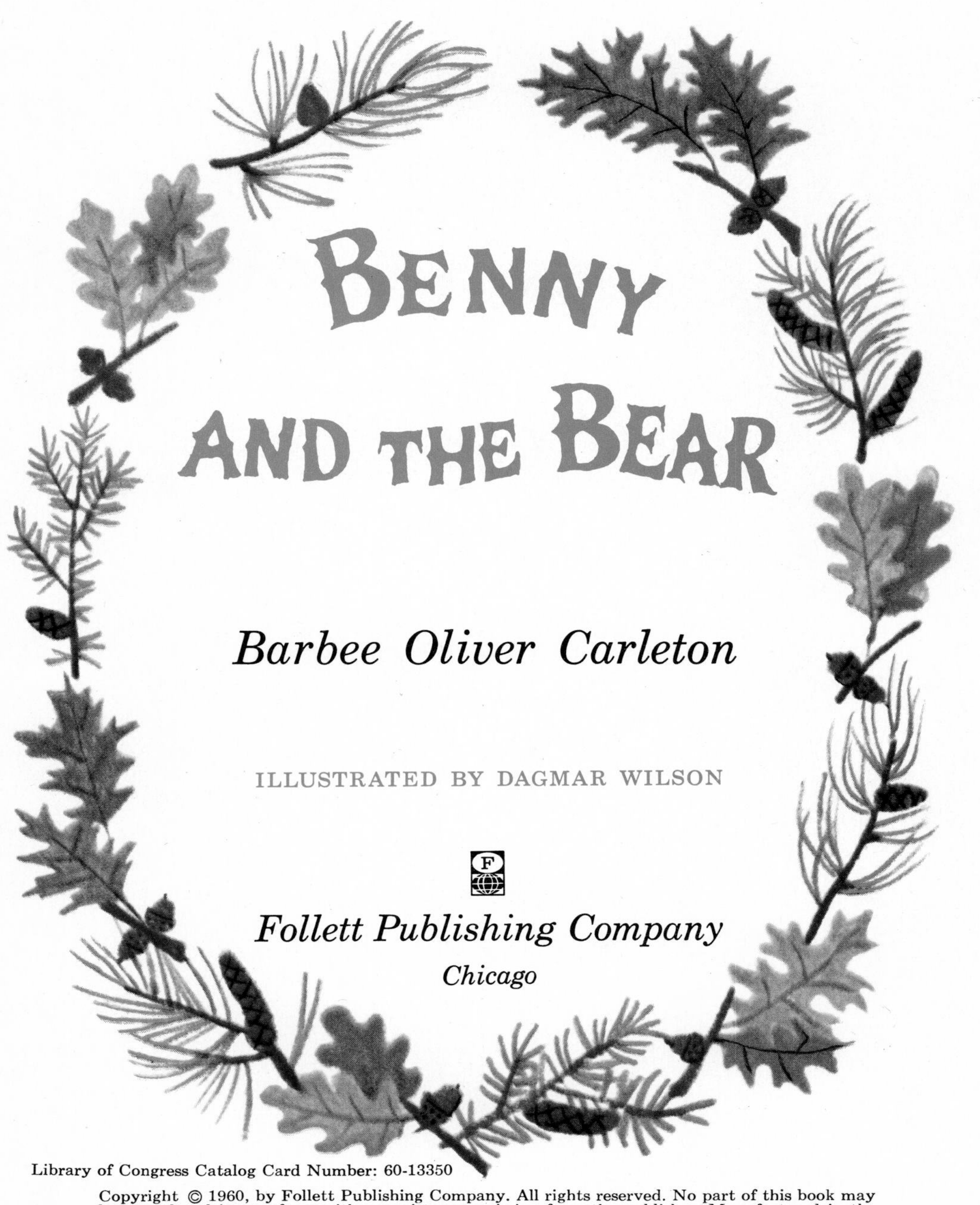

BENNY AND THE BEAR

Barbee Oliver Carleton

ILLUSTRATED BY DAGMAR WILSON

Follett Publishing Company

Chicago

Library of Congress Catalog Card Number: 60-13350

Benny had three good things.
He had a little house in the woods.

He had three brothers who were big and brave.

And Benny had a dream.

He dreamed of being as big and as brave as his brothers.

Now Benny was not very big, and he was not very brave.

So this was a good dream to have, and he had had it for a long time.

"Some day," thought Benny, "something will happen. Something DANGEROUS.

Then everybody will see how big and brave I am!"

But nothing happened. Day by day the brothers went into the woods.

Off they went to cut wood, as big and brave as ever.

And day by day Benny stayed at home and dreamed his dream.

He didn't get much bigger, and he didn't get any braver.

Then one day, something happened.

Some men with guns came to the house.

"A BEAR has come to the woods!" they cried.

"A bear!" said the brothers. "There hasn't been a bear in these woods for a long time!"

"It's a bear, all right," said the men. "A DANGEROUS bear!"

"We must get that bear," they said, "before he gets us!"

"We'll get him," said Benny's brothers.

And they got their guns.

Big and brave, they all started off into the woods.

All but Benny.

"Wait!" said Benny. "What about me?"

"You stay at home," said the brothers. "You wouldn't know a bear if you saw one."

"What does a bear look like?" asked Benny.

"What does a bear look like?"

The men laughed.

"Well, a bear is as big as a house.

He has terrible sharp teeth. And terrible strong claws. And a terrible, terrible loud roar. That's what a bear looks like," they whispered.

And they began to shake.

"Oh," said Benny. "So that's what a bear looks like."

He wished he were big enough and brave enough to get a bear.

"It's a good day to weed the corn," Benny said.

The cornfield was bright and sunny.

The woods beside the cornfield were big and dark.

As Benny looked they seemed to get bigger and darker.

"It is not a good day to weed corn," said Benny.

And he started for the house.

Just then something BIG came out of the woods.

It looked at Benny. Benny looked at it.

Benny thought of what the men had said about bears.

He thought of what a bear looked like.

"This is no bear," said Benny.

"Maybe it is a big brown dog," said Benny.

"Come, dog. Here, dog, dog, dog!"

The big brown dog came nearer. And nearer. And nearer.

With a terrible roar, the big brown dog stood up on his hind legs.

"Good boy!" said Benny.

He ran to the house for some meat for the dog.

But when he came back, the big brown dog had gone.

So Benny weeded the corn and dreamed his dream about being big and brave.

At supper time the brothers came home.

"Did you get the bear?" asked Benny.

"No," said the brothers.

"Oh," said Benny. Then, to cheer them up, he told them about the big brown dog.

"He's as smart as anything," said Benny.

"He comes when you call him. He can stand up. He can even speak!"

"Smart dog," said the brothers.

But Benny knew they were thinking about the bear.

In the morning the men came again. They had their guns and their axes.

"This time," said the men, "we shall set a trap for the bear."

"We must get that bear," a man said, "before he gets us!"

"We'll get him," said the brothers, and they got their guns and their axes.

Big and brave, they all started off into the woods. All but Benny.

"Wait!" said Benny. "What about me?"

"You stay at home," said the brothers. "You wouldn't know a bear if you saw one."

"Besides," said the men, "you have to be big and brave to get a bear.

Bears are dangerous!"

And they began to shake.

"Oh," said Benny. He wished that he were big enough and brave enough to get a bear.

He sat on the gate and watched them go.

Off they went into the woods to set a trap for the bear.

Benny went to weed the corn. He took along some meat in case the dog came back.

The cornfield was bright and sunny.

But the woods were big and black.

Benny began to think about what a bear looked like. Just then something big came out of the woods.

But it was only the big brown dog.

"Come, dog!" called Benny.

The big dog came nearer. And nearer. And nearer.

"Good dog," said Benny. "Now, speak!"

With a terrible roar, the big brown dog stood up on his hind legs.

"Good," said Benny, and tossed him some meat.

"Now," said Benny, "roll over."

The big brown dog did a good deal of roaring. He showed his teeth a good deal. But soon he could roll over like anything.

Soon he could chase sticks. And sit up and beg. And even play dead.

"A smart dog like this needs a collar," said Benny.

So he ran to the house for a collar.

But when he came back, the big brown dog was gone.

So Benny weeded the corn and dreamed his dream about being big and brave.

At supper time the brothers came home.

"Did you get the bear?" asked Benny.

"No," said the brothers.

"Oh," said Benny. To cheer them up, he told them about the big brown dog.

"Now he can roll over," said Benny.

"And chase sticks. And sit up and beg.
He can even play dead!"

"Smart dog," said the brothers.
But they were not thinking of dogs.
They were thinking about bears.

"We must get that bear," they said,
"before he gets us!"

In the morning the men came with their guns.

"This time," they said, "we shall track that bear. This time we shall follow his tracks until we find him."

"Then we shall shoot him," said the brothers. "And that will be that."

Big and brave, they all started off into the woods. All but Benny.

"Wait!" said Benny. "What about me?"

"You stay at home," said the brothers. "Today we shall get that bear."

Off they went into the woods to track the bear. Benny sat on the gate and watched them go.

He knew that today they would get the bear. Or the bear would get them.

So Benny went to weed the corn. He took along some meat and a collar in case the dog came back.

This time the big brown dog came straight out of the woods. He came straight to Benny.

Benny laughed. He patted his dog on his big brown head. He looked into his big soft eyes. He put on his collar and gave him some meat.

All that day they played together, Benny and his dog.

Not once did Benny think of the dangerous bear that was in the woods. Not once did he dream about being big and brave.

Then all at once, something moved in the woods. It came nearer and nearer.

Benny's dog stood up on his hind legs. He gave a terrible roar.

Benny got behind his dog. "The bear is coming!" he whispered.

But a bear did not come out of the woods. Out of the woods came Benny's brothers and the men.

"The bear!" they cried.

"Where?" they cried.

"There!" they cried.

"Get him before he gets us!" they cried.

And they pointed their guns straight at Benny's dog. "Shoot!"

"Stop!" cried Benny. "Don't shoot!" And he put his arms around the big brown dog.

"Benny!" cried the brothers. "Get out of the way!"

"Don't shoot my dog!" cried Benny, staying where he was.

"Dog nothing!" cried the men. "That's a BEAR!"

Benny looked at the bear. The bear looked back at Benny with his big soft eyes.

"Get out of the way, Benny!" said the men. "We're going to shoot!"

All at once Benny began to feel big and brave. He stood between the men and the bear.

"Play dead," said Benny to the bear. The bear played dead.

"Roll over," said Benny. The bear rolled over. He shook hands.

He did everything that Benny told him to do. He licked Benny's face, besides.

Then Benny said to the men, "You can't shoot this bear. This is my bear."

The men put down their guns.
"Well, what do you know!" said the men.

"Benny," said his brothers,
"you have tamed a bear!"

"You can sell him," said the men,
coming a little nearer (but not much).
"You can make a good deal of money."

Benny thought it over. "No,
thank you," he said. "I don't need money
half so much as I need this bear."

Then, big and brave, Benny and his
bear went home to supper.